CBeebies
BBC

One day, Fimbo and Rockit saw a little rain cloud drift into Fimble Valley.

"Tippity toppity!" shouted Rockit. "Today I'm pretending to be a flower, and flowers need rain. Rain on me, little rain cloud!"

The little rain cloud rained on Rockit.
"Smelly jelly!" said Rockit.
"It's cold and wet! Stop!"

Then the little
rain cloud rained
on Fimbo.

"Don't rain on me, little rain cloud!" said Fimbo. "I'm not
a flower!" The little rain cloud drifted sadly away.

9

On the other side of Fimble Valley, the Tinkling Tree had started tinkling. "Fimbly Feeling!" cried Baby Pom.

"Feel a twinkling,
Hear a sound, It's something
Waiting to be found!
Where is it? Where is it?
What could it be?
Something over there,
Let's go and see!"

Baby Pom and Florrie found something long and thin hanging on a tree.

"Look, Florrie!" cried Baby Pom. The long thing opened up to become a wide thing with a long wooden handle.

"Let's ask Bessie what it is," said Florrie.

"Oh, that's a fine umbrella you've got there, Pom," said Bessie. "You use an umbrella to keep you dry when it's raining."

Baby Pom loved her new umbrella. She wanted it to rain, so that she could use her umbrella straight away.

But there were no rain clouds anywhere in the sky above Fimble Valley.

"No rain for Pom!" sighed Baby Pom.
"Pom not happy. Pom sad!"

"What's the matter, Pom?" asked Fimbo.

"Pom want rain," said Baby Pom.
"Pom go sit on dreamstone and wait for rain."

19

"There was a little rain cloud here earlier," said Fimbo to Florrie, "but I think it went away, because Rockit and I told it not to rain on us."

"We've got to find that rain cloud!" said Florrie.

"Little rain cloud!" called Florrie.

"Little rain cloud!" called Fimbo.

22

"Have you seen
the little rain cloud
again, Rockit?"
asked Fimbo.

"Glung! No!"
glunged Rockit.

23

"Have you seen a
little rain cloud, Roly?"
asked Florrie.

"Sorry, Florrie,
I haven't,"
said Roly Mo.

24

"We'll never find that rain cloud," said Florrie to Fimbo.

But just then, Fimbo felt a drop of rain.

The little rain cloud was hiding behind a rock. "I'm sorry for telling you not to rain on me, little rain cloud," said Fimbo. "Will you rain on Pom, little rain cloud?" asked Florrie. "Please?"

The little rain cloud
drifted over Baby Pom...
and started to rain.

Patter patter went
the raindrops on
Baby Pom's umbrella.

"Rain!" cried
Baby Pom.
"Thank you,
little rain cloud!"

And both Baby Pom
and the little rain cloud
were very happy.

28

Tweenies™

Make It Big!

Milo and Jake had a problem. They were building the castle of Sir Milo the Great, but there was a big hole in the wall.

"Could you pass me some bricks to put in here, please, Jake?" Milo asked.

Jake took one out of the box.

"No mate, I wanted one to fill this space," said Milo. "That one's too small."

Jake looked in the box.

"Sorry, Milo, but there aren't any big enough bricks to fill that space."

Milo sighed. How was he going to finish the castle?

On the other side of the room, Max had a problem, too. He, Fizz and Bella were taking some old pictures off the wall and there were large dark marks where the pictures had been.

"We're going to need something pretty big to cover up these marks," said Max.

Jake came over to watch.

"How's the castle, Jake?" asked Bella.

"We've run out of big bricks," he explained. Then he looked up.

"Eeurgh! Look at those big marks on the wall.

You'd better cover them up with something, Max!"

Judy was showing Milo how to
finish the castle when Jake got back.

"Look, Jakey! The castle of Sir Milo the Great is now finished!" said Milo.

"Wow! How did you do that?" asked Jake in surprise.

"Judy showed me how three little bricks can fill the same space as one big one," Milo explained.

That reminded Jake and Milo of a song they knew. Bella and Fizz joined in.

There are hundreds of grains of sand on a beach,
Thousands of hairs on your head.
Can you count all the bricks in the walls of your house?
Or the bubbles in your bath before bed?

Take a look at the world around us,
At the things that we use and we see.
There are so many things made from smaller things.
Come and look at some more with me.

How many pieces make up an orange?
How many trees in a wood?
Can you count all the blades of grass in a field?
You'd find millions of them if you could.

Lots of petals make up a flower,
  Hundreds of sticks make a nest.
How many crumbs in a piece of cake?
  I like counting those up the best!

So, take a look at the world around us,
At the things that we use and we see.
There are so many things made from smaller things.
Spot some more and show them to me.

The Tweenies started to look around.

"A jigsaw puzzle is made of lots of small bits!" said Fizz.

"And lots of little beads make up this necklace," shouted Bella.

"And my huge lunch is made up of lots of big sandwiches!" laughed Milo.

"And castles are made with lots of bricks," added Jake.

"That's given me an idea," said Max.

Max called the Tweenies over to the messy table. There were piles of tiny squares of coloured paper. Max put a big sheet of plain paper on the floor and started to explain.

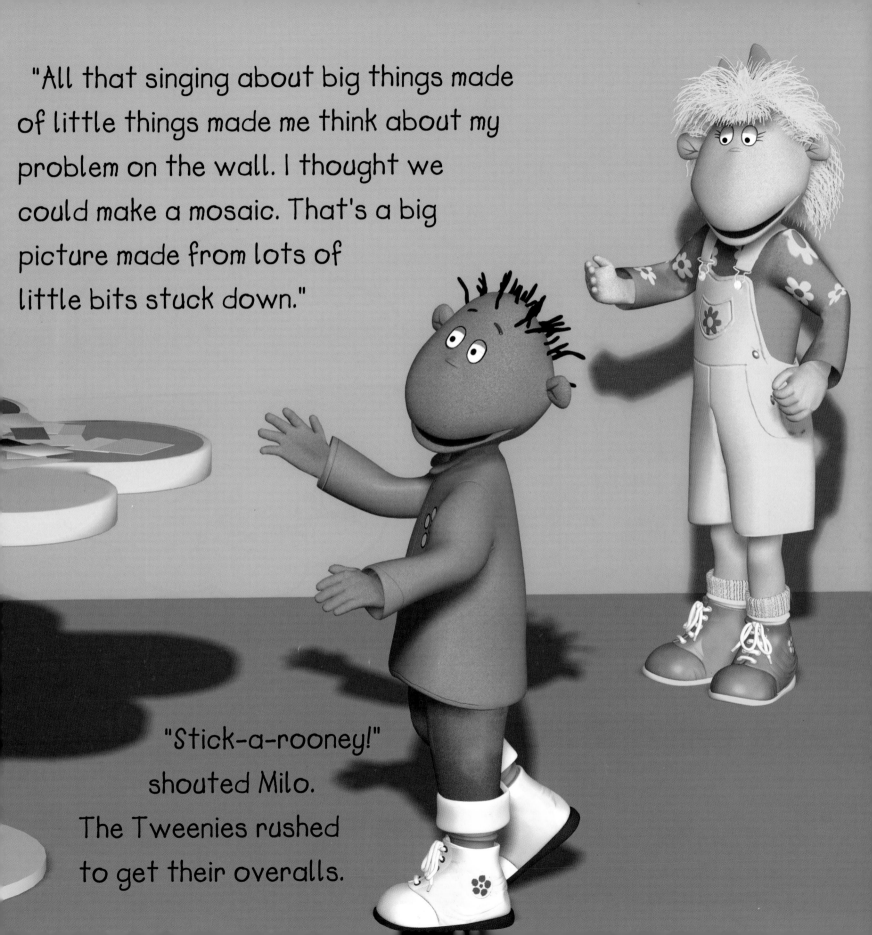

"All that singing about big things made of little things made me think about my problem on the wall. I thought we could make a mosaic. That's a big picture made from lots of little bits stuck down."

"Stick-a-rooney!" shouted Milo. The Tweenies rushed to get their overalls.

"All we need to do now is decide what the picture will be," said Max.

Milo wanted to do a castle, of course.

Jake liked the idea of the seaside.

44

Fizz wanted a fairy grotto and Bella wanted a house.
In the end, they agreed to make a picture that everyone
would like.

"You can each have your own corner to decorate,"
Max promised.

Judy told the Tweenies where to put the different colours.

"That's right, Jake. You need lots of red and yellow bits," she said. She helped Bella, Milo and Fizz with their sticking, too.

Doodles tried to help them but he got bits of paper stuck all over him, so Judy had to clean him up. Doodles wasn't the only one getting in a mess. Soon there was paper everywhere!

Finally, the Tweenies put down their gluing brushes and stood up to have a look.

"It's fantastic!" gasped Bella.

"And it's huge!" said Milo.

The paper was filled from end to end. Everyone had helped to make a really special picture.

"Excellent!" said Max. "Now let's see what it looks like on the wall."

"Oh, we've made a great big Doodles," said Jake.

"And it fits over those big marks!" said Fizz.

50

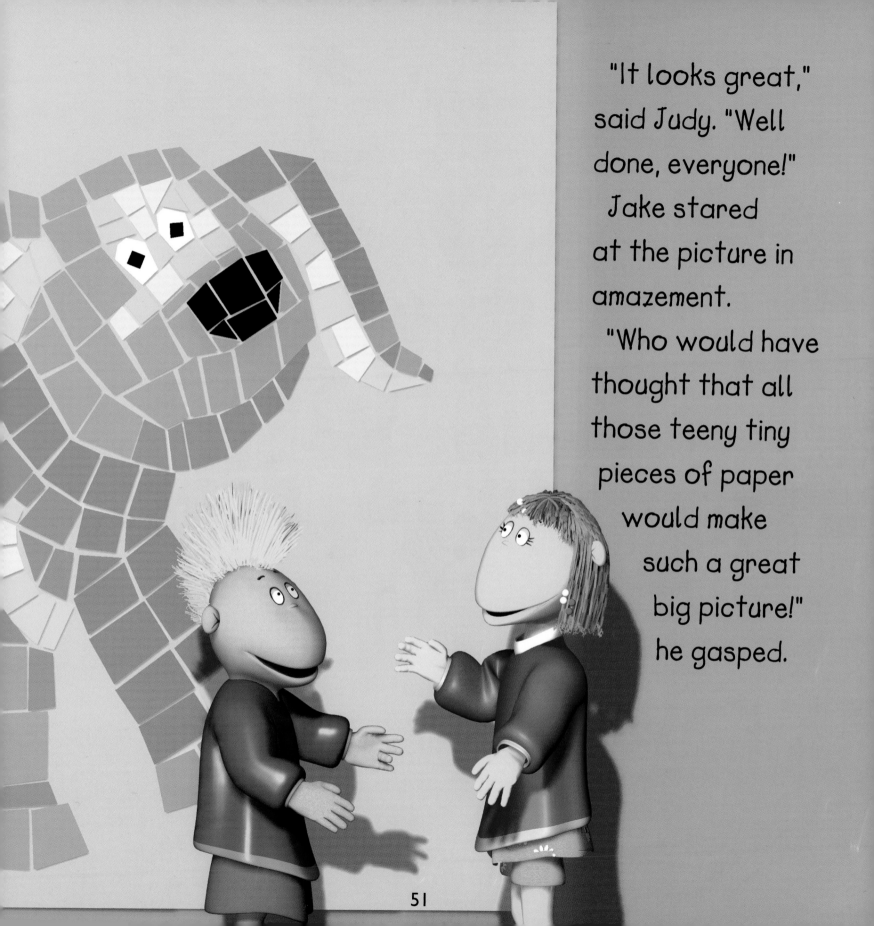

"It looks great," said Judy. "Well done, everyone!" Jake stared at the picture in amazement.

"Who would have thought that all those teeny tiny pieces of paper would make such a great big picture!" he gasped.

51

"And such a huge, sticky mess!" said Judy.

THE END

Sunglasses

It was a hot and sunny day,
and everyone had been having an
afternoon nap. Andy Pandy and
Looby Loo were going to have a
picnic with their friends.

Andy Pandy went to his fridge and got
the lemonade he had made.

But there was something missing. Straws!
He went to get a box of straws from his
special cupboard.

He was surprised to find a pair of sunglasses
in there, too.

Andy Pandy thought the sunglasses were just
what he needed on such a sunny day.

Andy Pandy carried the lemonade into the garden.

When Teddy saw Andy Pandy's sunglasses,
he said that he wanted a pair just like them.
Andy Pandy said that he was sorry, but he only
had one pair.

Andy Pandy and Looby Loo called their friends into the garden for the picnic.

Everyone felt too hot to eat Looby Loo's
sandwiches, but they all wanted some of
Andy Pandy's cool lemonade.

Teddy had decided to make his own sunglasses.
There was only one thing wrong: they were
made from black cardboard, so he couldn't see
through them!

Teddy knocked over his table and chairs.
Then he staggered into the garden.

Teddy tried to join the picnic, but he couldn't see through his cardboard sunglasses.

First the swing got in the way.

Then the picnic basket got in the way.
Careful, Teddy!

Andy Pandy sat Teddy down. He asked Teddy
if they could swap sunglasses.

Now Andy Pandy couldn't *see* anything!
Careful, Andy Pandy!

Andy Pandy explained to Teddy that sunglasses were made of glass, so you could see through them. The glass was dark, to make the sunlight seem less bright. Just as he finished...

...the sun went in. No one needed to wear sunglasses any more. It was much cooler. Now everyone wanted to eat Looby Loo's sandwiches.

Teddy said that he thought sandwiches were much better than sunglasses. Wearing sunglasses, said Teddy, had been very difficult indeed.

Four Happy Teletubbies

One day in Teletubbyland,

all the Teletubbies were feeling
very, very happy.

Four happy Teletubbies jumping round a tree.

Happy Teletubbies!

One jumped away

Jumpy, jumpy, jump!

and then there were ...

three!

Three happy Teletubbies.
What did they do?

One went to hide

and then there were ...

two!

One... two!

Two happy
Teletubbies out
for a run.

Faster and faster

and then there was ...

one!

One happy
Teletubby sitting
in the sun ...

rolled right away

and then there were ...

none!

Where have all the Teletubbies gone?

One happy Teletubby playing peek-a-boo!

Eh-oh!

Along came another

and then there were ...

two!

Two happy
Teletubbies.
What did
they see?

They saw another Teletubby

and then there were ...

three!

Three happy Teletubbies.
Are there any more?

Of course there are

so then there were ...

four!

One!

Two!

Three!

Four!

Four happy Teletubbies.
What a happy game and Teletubbies
want to play again and again.

Again!

Teletubbies love each other very much.

Bye-bye

Little Robots™

Sporty Takes Off

Tiny pulled the Day-Night
Lever, and it was morning.
Sporty was exercising, Rusty
was gardening, and Stretchy was
waiting for a delivery of junk.

When Stretchy
opened the junk chute,
two enormous magnets fell out.
Clunk! Clunk!
And stuck to him.
Clang! Clang!

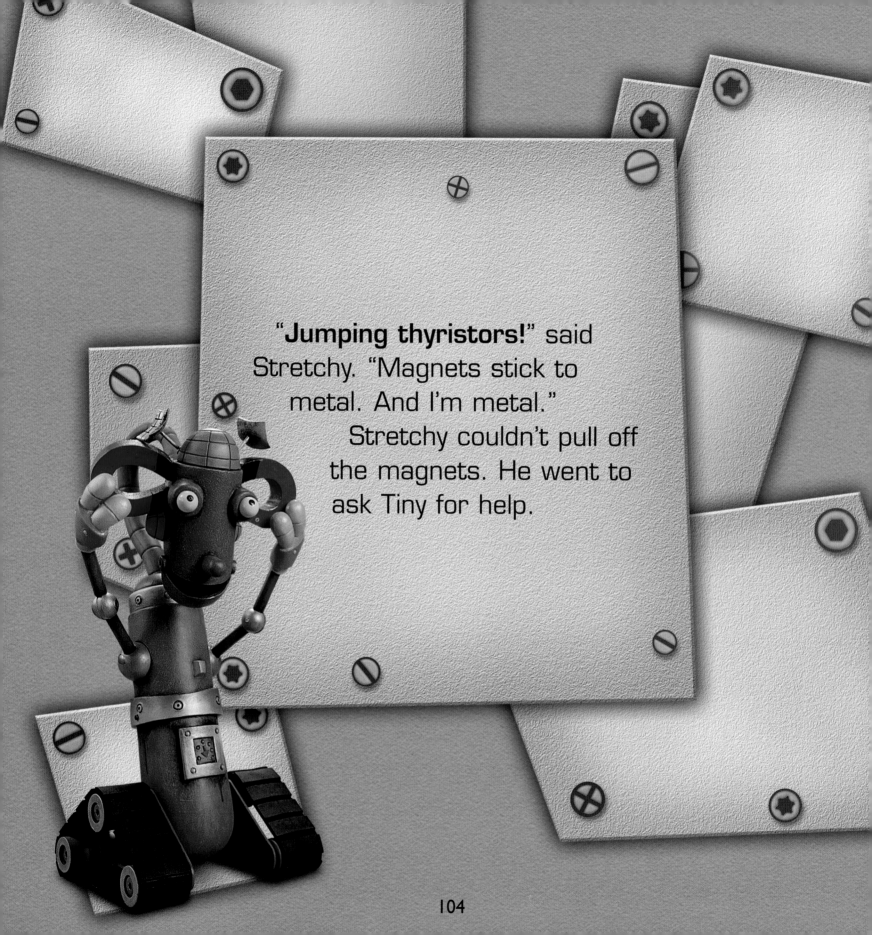

"**Jumping thyristors!**" said Stretchy. "Magnets stick to metal. And I'm metal."
Stretchy couldn't pull off the magnets. He went to ask Tiny for help.

Together, Tiny and Stretchy
pulled the magnets off.

But something strange
happened. When Stretchy and
Tiny tried to put the magnets
together, they pushed each
other away.

"Fascinating," said Stretchy.
"These magnets push as
well as stick!" He used
his magnet to push
Tiny gently away.

Not far away, Sporty was
running happily on the spot.
"**Hup! Hup! Hup!**" he said
to himself. "I love running."
Then a Robobird flew by.
"Tweet tweet!"
"Hmm," said Sporty.
"I love running. But I
think I'd love flying
even more."

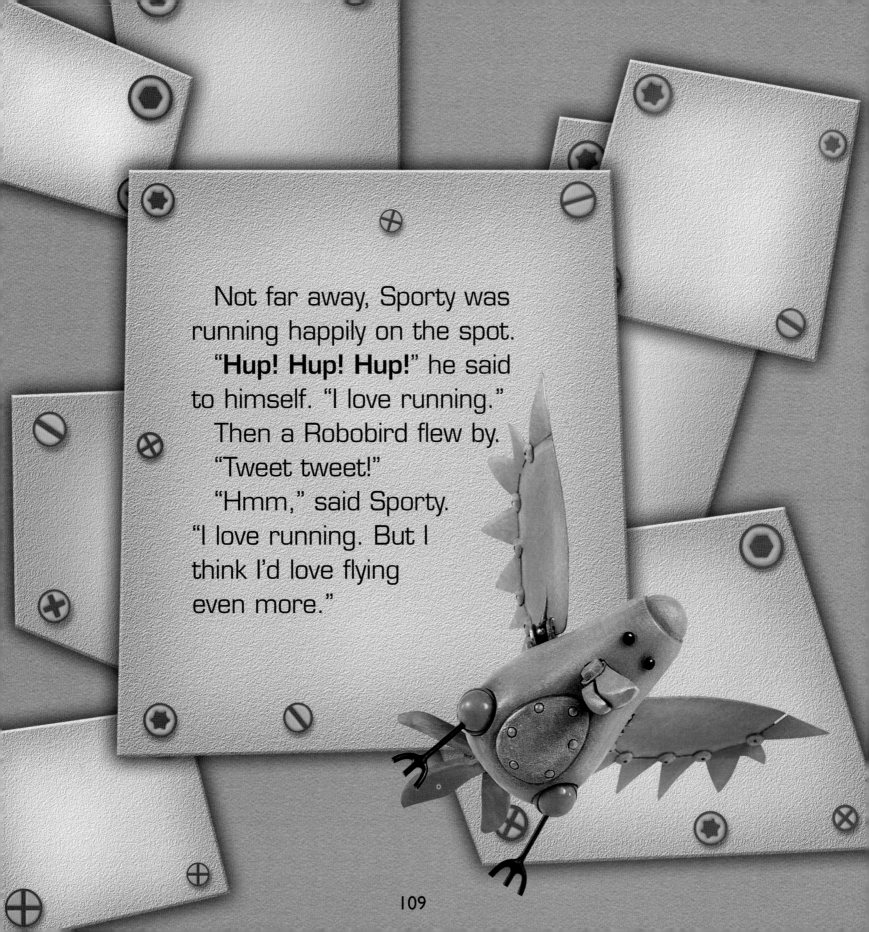

Sporty flapped his
arms. Nothing happened.
"Why not?" he wondered.
"A little Robobird can fly.
It shouldn't be hard for a big,
strong robot like me."

He flapped his arms harder. Still nothing happened.
Sporty stopped to think.

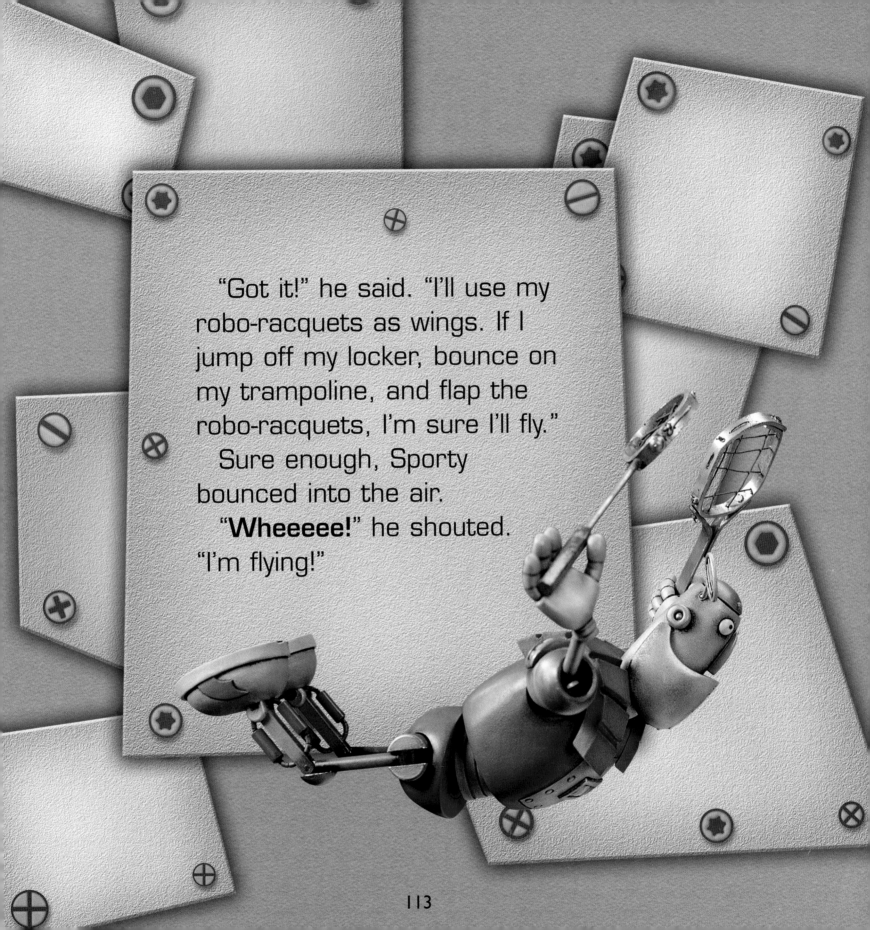

"Got it!" he said. "I'll use my robo-racquets as wings. If I jump off my locker, bounce on my trampoline, and flap the robo-racquets, I'm sure I'll fly."

Sure enough, Sporty bounced into the air.

"**Wheeeee!**" he shouted. "I'm flying!"

Sporty flew over
Rusty's garden.
Then Rusty heard a loud
crash. She found Sporty on top
of a stack in the wasteland.

"What happened?"
she asked.
"I was trying to fly,"
replied Sporty.

Rusty looked worried.
"Is that a good idea?" she asked.
"It would be," said Sporty,
"if I knew how."
Then Sporty had an
amazing idea.

"Let's make a helicopter!" he said. "I'll wrap an elastic band round my head. Then you can thread a lollipop stick through it."

"Now what?" asked Rusty.
"Turn the lollipop stick round
and round and round, then
let go," boomed Sporty.
Sporty spun around and
fell over.

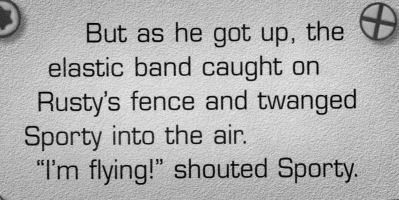

But as he got up, the elastic band caught on Rusty's fence and twanged Sporty into the air.
"I'm flying!" shouted Sporty.

Stretchy and Tiny were
still playing with their magnets
when they heard a noise overhead.
Sporty crashed down in front
of them. "**Ouch!**" he said.

"That wasn't supposed to happen."

"What was supposed to happen?" asked Tiny.

"I'm trying to fly," replied Sporty.

Tiny thought.

"I know," he said. "Let's fix one magnet on to Stretchy's junk cart, and use the magnetic power to push the other magnet into the air."

Tiny told Sporty to climb on top of the floating magnet.

Then Stretchy pulled the junk cart along.

"**Wow!**" shouted Sporty. "I really am flying!"

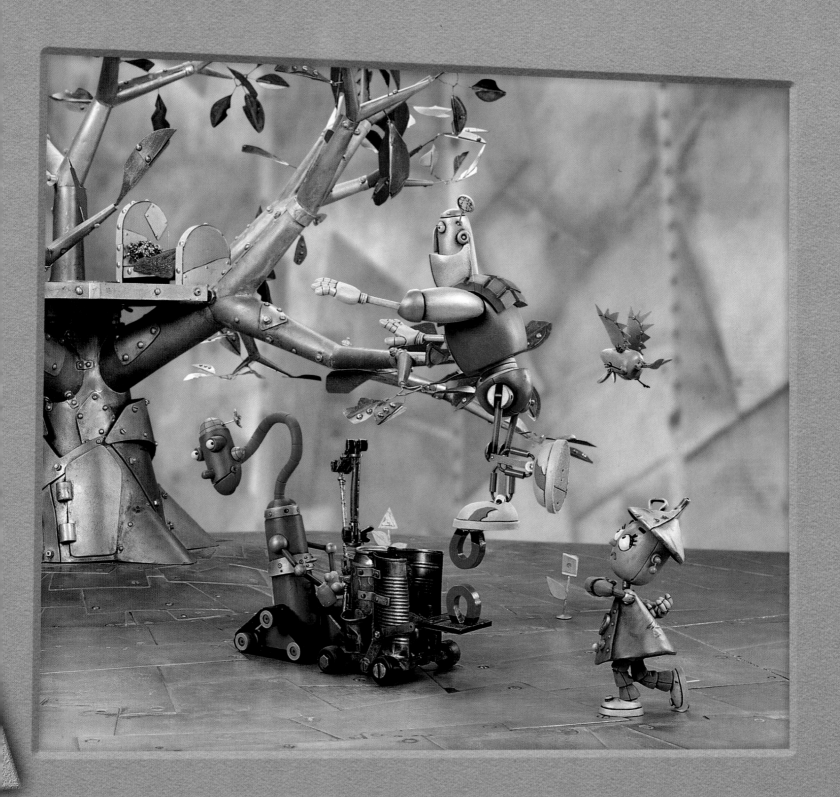

123

"How does it feel?"
called Rusty.
"**Great!**" said Sporty.
"Just like being a Robobird!"

The End

Stinky Pingu

Pingu and Pinga were waiting for their breakfast.

126

Mother brought them each a big, steaming bowl of fish porridge.

Pinga thought the
porridge was yummy, but
Pingu didn't like it.

Mother told Pingu that he was not to leave the table until he had eaten it all up.

But when she left the room, Pingu poured the porridge into his bag, and went out to play.

Pingu thought
that Robby
might like the
fish porridge,
but Robby said
it smelt horrible.

Robby said they should have a food fight with the porridge.

The bag flew up into the air...

and landed with a plop on Pingu's head.

Robby said that he didn't want to play with such a smelly penguin.

On the way home, Pingu tripped and fell head first into a rubbish bin. It was not a good day.

Poor stinky
Pingu! Nobody
would go
anywhere
near him.

139

Even Mother and Father kept away from him.

Pinga thought Pingu was far too smelly
to share her bath, but he jumped
in anyway.

Then Pinga made a stinky smell of her own…

Yuk! Pingu leapt back out of the bath.

Mother helped Pinga out too,
and got them ready
for dinner.

Oh no! It was
fish porridge
again!

But
Mother
said she had
a surprise in the
oven for Pingu.

A lovely big fish, just for him.

And it didn't smell at all!

Fimbo's Teddy

It was afternoon
nap time in
Fimble Valley.

"Sleep tight, Pom!
Sleep tight, Fimbo!"
yawned Florrie,
snuggling up with Little
One and closing her eyes.

"Sleepy tightly, you ones!" yawned Baby Pom, snuggling up with her pink blanket and closing her eyes.

"Sleep tight, everyone!" said Fimbo.
But Fimbo's eyes just wouldn't close.

Fimbo wasn't sleepy at all. He was wide awake.

Fimbo went to see if Rockit could help him go to sleep.

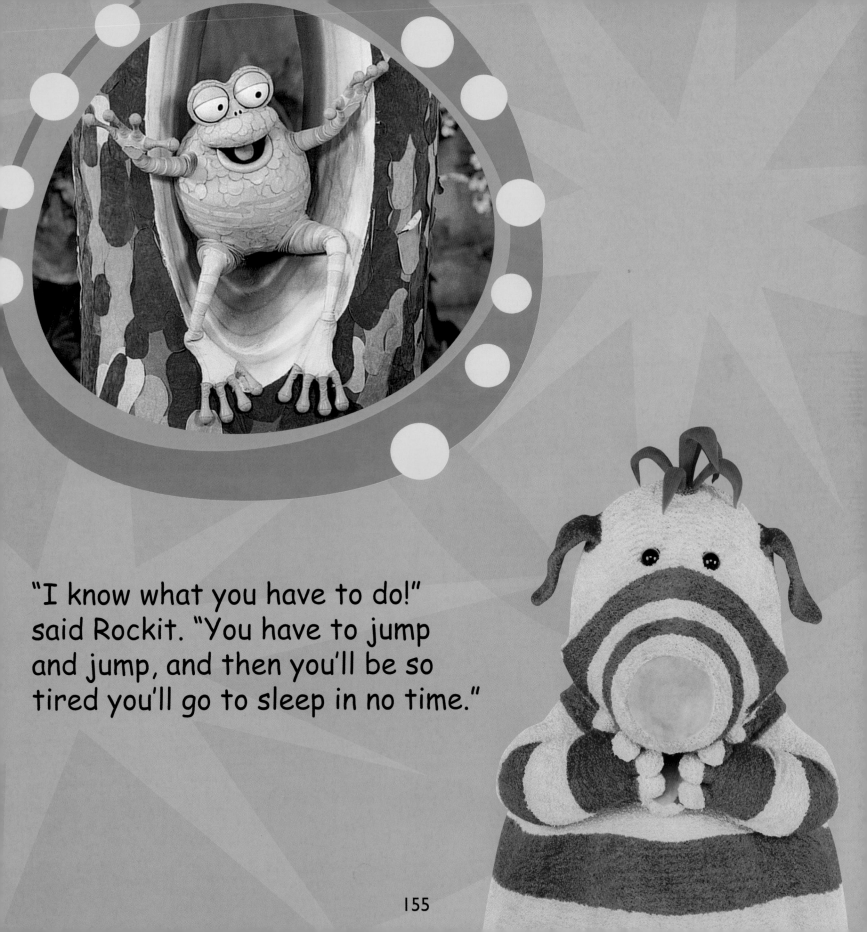

"I know what you have to do!"
said Rockit. "You have to jump
and jump, and then you'll be so
tired you'll go to sleep in no time."

155

Fimbo and Rockit jumped high and low and left and right. They jumped until they couldn't jump any more.

"Smelly jelly!" yawned Rockit. "All that jumping has made me very sleepy!" Rockit's eyes started to close...

But Fimbo's eyes were still wide open. He went to see if Roly Mo could help him go to sleep.

"Perhaps a sleepytime story
will help you fall asleep,"
said Roly Mo.

"Are you sleepy now, Fimbo?" said Roly Mo, when he had finished reading the story. "I know I am!"

Fimbo tried to close his eyes, but he was still wide awake.

"Sometimes I find that counting things helps me go to sleep," said Roly Mo.

"What could I count?" wondered Fimbo.

161

"I know! I'll count Crumble Crackers, because they're one of my favourite things." One Crumble Cracker... two Crumble Crackers... three Crumble Crackers...

But counting Crumble Crackers didn't make Fimbo sleepy.
It made him **HUNGRY**.

"I can't go to sleep if I'm hungry!" said Fimbo. "I'll have to go and get a Crumble Cracker from the barrel."

On the way to the Busy Base, Fimbo started to get a special feeling...

"I can feel a twinkling,
I can hear a sound,
It's telling me there's something
Waiting to be found!
Where is it? Where is it?
What could it be?
I think it might be over there,
Let's go and see!"

Fimbo found something small and furry in the Playdips.

"I wonder what it is?" he said.
"It looks a bit like Little One, but it's not a doll."

"Hello Fimbo!" chirped Bessie. "Are you still awake?
Ooh, look what you've found!
A teddy bear!"

"I can't get to sleep, Bessie," sighed Fimbo.

"You poor little sausage!" said Bessie. "But do you know, I think this teddy might help. Cuddling a soft toy, like a teddy bear, can help you fall asleep."

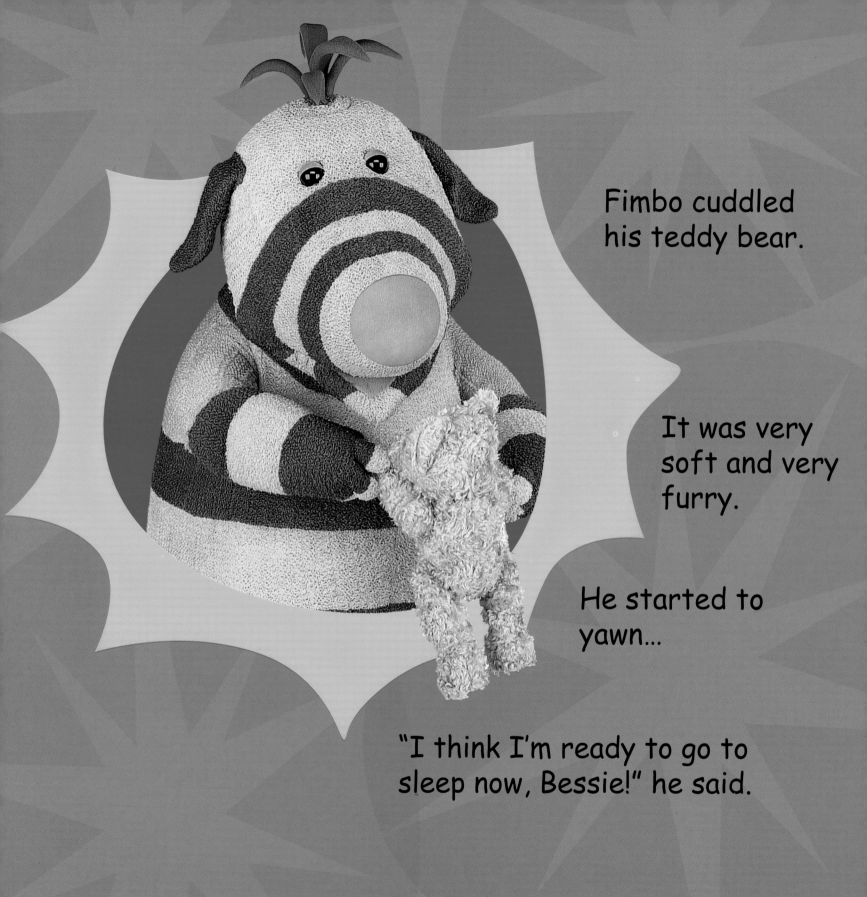

Fimbo cuddled his teddy bear.

It was very soft and very furry.

He started to yawn...

"I think I'm ready to go to sleep now, Bessie!" he said.

"Sleep tight, everyone! Sleep tight, teddy!" yawned Fimbo, snuggling up with his new teddy and closing his eyes.

And at long last, everyone in Fimble Valley was...

...asleep!

Spud's Campfire

It was a bright sunny day in Sunflower Valley. Bob and the machines were ready to start work at the new base.

Spud was hiding in Bob's mobile home.

"Sunflowers!" he said, looking around. "Is that all there is here?"

"Adventures, too!"
said Muck.

"Camping adventures?
With food I hope?" asked
Spud, eagerly.

"Let's have a camping adventure *tonight*," said Bob. "Muck and Spud, off you go to collect branches to make a real campfire."

And off they went into the forest.

After a little while, it started to get dark.

"Let's go back now, Spud," said Muck. "There's plenty of firewood here."

Muck was afraid of the dark but he didn't want to tell Spud.

But Spud went deeper into the dark forest to find some bigger branches.

Muck felt frightened on his own. "Wait for me, Spud!" he called.

"Lots of lovely firewood,"
Spud sang, "...to cook
Spuddy a yummy dinner!"

Just then, a squawking noise
came from the forest. It made
Muck jump.

"Aaargh! Spud! What was that?" cried Muck.

"It's just a silly bird," said Spud. "Come on, there's nothing to be frightened about!"

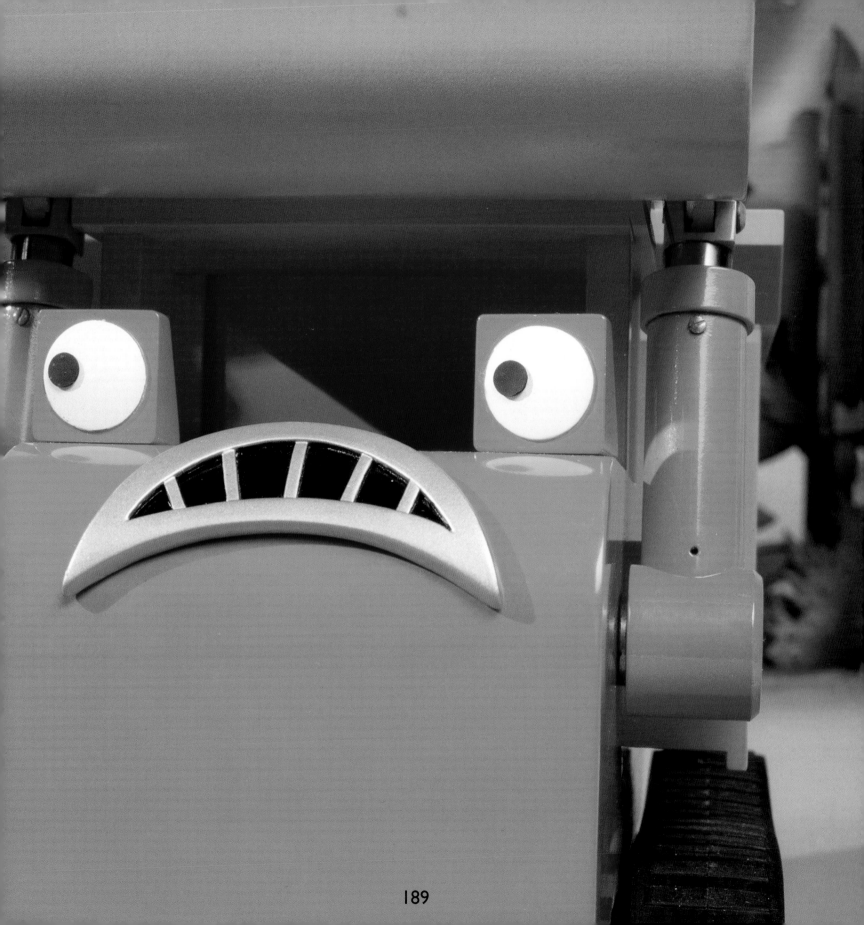

189

Just then a rustling noise came from the forest.

"Oooh! Muck! What was that?" cried Spud.

"It's just some badgers!" said Muck. "Come on, let's go and find Bob."

When they got to the camp, Muck and Spud told everyone about their adventure in the forest.

"It's all right, Muck," said Bob. "We can all feel a bit frightened in a new place. Let's get the campfire going, everyone."

Bob made delicious hot toast on the campfire.

"Foooood! Yummy!" Spud cried, eating it all at once.

"Spud!" cried Bob.

"Ooops, sorry!" he said. "I was sooo hungry after my campfire adventure!"

And they all laughed.

Scary Finbar

Finbar was sneaking
up on Tubb and Terence.
"Little do they know
they're about to get the
fright of their lives!"
he grinned. "**BOO!**"

But Tubb just said,
"Hi, Finbar! Want to
play volleyball?"

"The mighty shark will just have to find someone else to scare," muttered Finbar.

He saw Winona and Reg sleeping.

"BOO!"

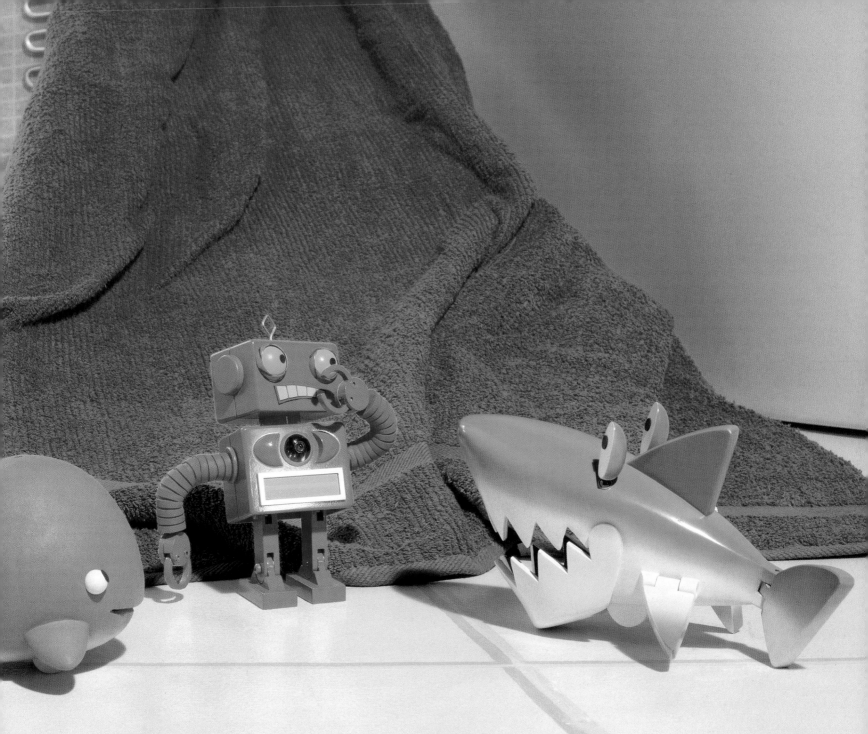

But Reg just said, "Thanks for waking us up,
Finbar. I should be on lookout!"

"You're supposed to be scared of me!"
snapped Finbar, gnashing his teeth.
Winona gave a friendly squeak.

"**If only** everyone were really scared of me," imagined Finbar.
And something amazing began to happen...

Finbar found himself gliding through the sea towards Sploshy and Tubb.

"**BOO!**" roared Finbar.

"**Aaaargh!** It's the mighty scary shark!" shouted Tubb. "He wants to eat us!" They jumped out of the sea and ran off to hide.

Finbar saw Amelia and Winona on the beach.

205

He leapt out of the sea. "**BOO!**"
"**Aaaargh!**" they squealed, running off to hide. "It's the mighty
scary shark!"

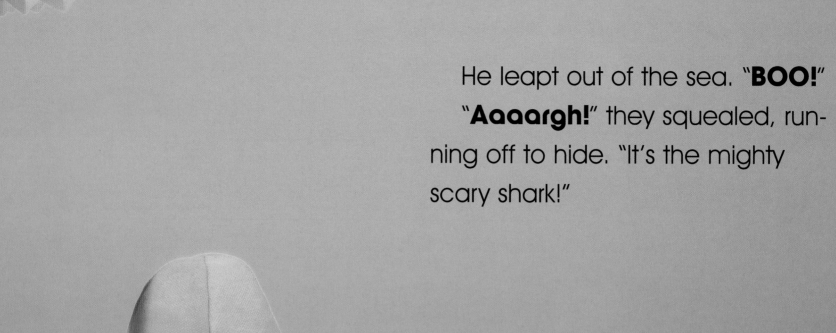

"This is great!" laughed Finbar.
"Who can the mighty shark
scare next?"

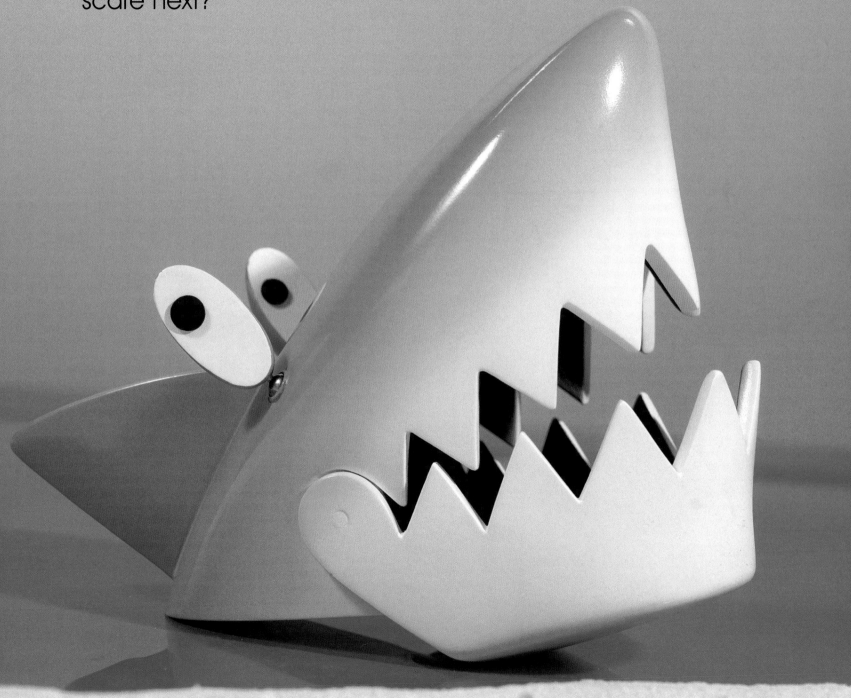

Terence was tangled in a volleyball net.

"He looks like he needs help," said Finbar.

"First I'll help him – then I'll scare him!"

"**Aaaargh!** It's the m-m-mighty scary shark!" yelled Terence.

"Right now I just want to be mighty helpful,"
said Finbar, gripping the net in his teeth.

"Don't eat me!" cried Terence, running off.

Tubb and Sploshy were hiding from the mighty shark behind a tree, but there wasn't enough room for Terence as well.

Terence ran to the beach hut.
"There's no spa… there's no spa…
there's no room here!" said Reg,
shutting the door.

"Wait!" shouted Finbar to Terence.
"I want to help you!"

Then Finbar saw himself in a rock pool. "**Aaaargh!**" he cried. "Another mighty scary shark!"

"Er… Mr Shark?" said Terence "It's your reflection."

214

"Ah," said Finbar. "No wonder everyone's scared. I look like I want to eat someone!"

"Don't you want to eat us?" asked Terence.

"Of course not," said Finbar. "You're my friends."

"Then you're not really scary, are you?" asked Reg.

"I suppose not…" said Finbar. "But being scary wasn't as much fun as the mighty shark thought. Now, **if only** I could untangle Terence, we could play volleyball…"

In the blink of an eye…

...they were all back in the bathroom.

"I wonder if I'm still scary?" thought Finbar.
"BOO!"
"Aaaargh!"
shouted Terence.
"Oh, no!" said Finbar.

218

"Only joking," said Terence. "I thought you wanted to be scary."

219

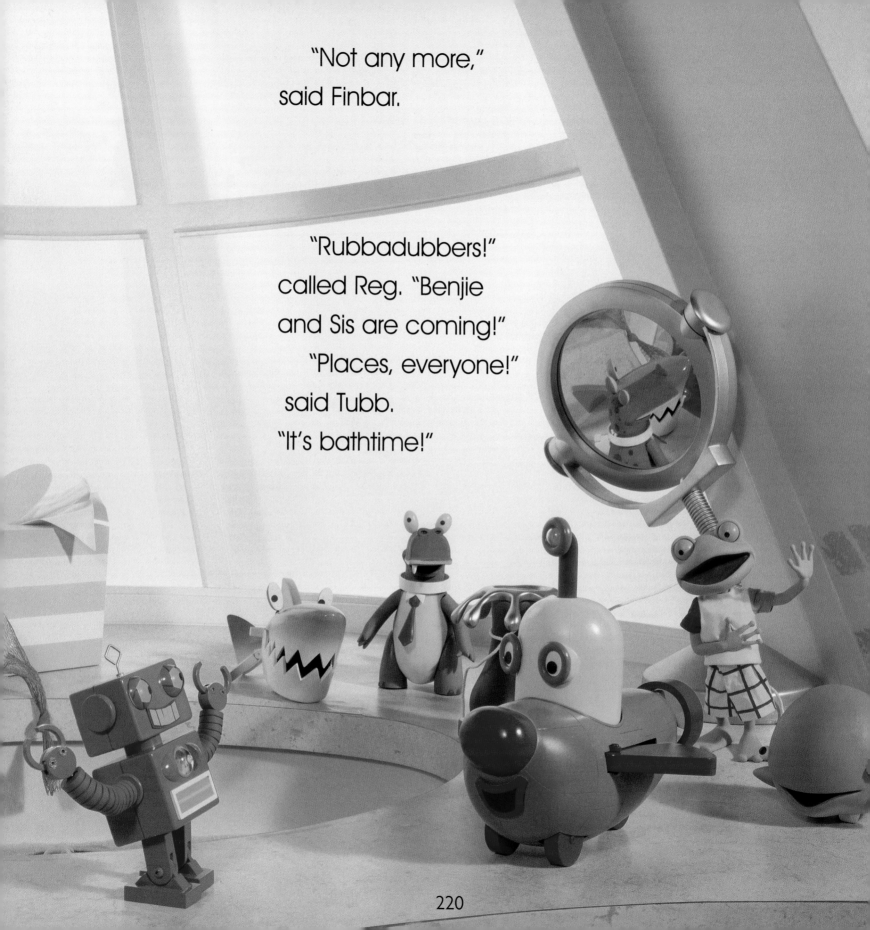

"Not any more,"
said Finbar.

"Rubbadubbers!"
called Reg. "Benjie
and Sis are coming!"
"Places, everyone!"
said Tubb.
"It's bathtime!"

Tweenies™

The Wobbly
Jelly Hunt

One day, the Tweenies wanted to make something that they all liked to eat.

"Oh, can we make jelly?" asked Fizz. "I like jelly."

"Me too," agreed Milo.

"That's a good idea," said Max. "You can each have a different flavour. And we can add some fruit, too. I've got raspberries, strawberries, oranges and blackcurrants."

"Mmmm. Fruit jellies! I like the sound of those," said Jake, excitedly. The Tweenies couldn't wait to start.

Max opened a packet of raspberry jelly and showed Bella how to mix the jelly with some warm water.
"That's right, Bella. Just stir it a bit with that spoon," said Max.

"What shall
I do, Max?"
asked Jake.

"Choose a
flavour, Jake,
and I'll show you
how to make your jelly."

Jake chose strawberry
and mixed the jelly with water,
just like Bella had done.

"Oh, can I have orange
flavour?" asked Fizz, excitedly.

"I suppose I'll have to have
the blackcurrant then,
because it's the only one
left," said Milo.

Soon, the Tweenies were ready to pour the jellies into their moulds.

"Now we can add the fruit," said Max.

Bella added some raspberries to her jelly. Jake added some strawberries to his. Fizz put orange segments in her jelly and Milo sprinkled lots of blackcurrants into his.

Then Max put the jellies in the fridge.

"Mmmm, I'm hungry. Can we eat the jellies now?" asked Fizz.

"We've got to let them set first," said Max.

"But I want to taste one now!" said Bella, crossly.

"Me, too!" said Milo and Jake at the same time.

Max explained that the
jellies would be soft if
they tried to eat them now.

"Jelly should be wobbly,
not runny," said Max.

The Tweenies looked very
disappointed.

"I can't wait much longer,"
said Jake, rubbing his tummy.

"Neither can I," agreed Bella.

"Nor me," said Fizz.

"What can we do while
we're waiting?" asked Milo
with a sigh.

Then Max had an idea.

"I know," he said. "You can
go on a treasure hunt!"

Max explained.
"I'm going to give you some clues and you have to find the treasure," he said with a smile.

"That sounds like fun, Max," said Fizz. "Maybe we'll find gold and jewels."

"Let's get ready!" said Milo, and the Tweenies took off their overalls while Max prepared the first clue.

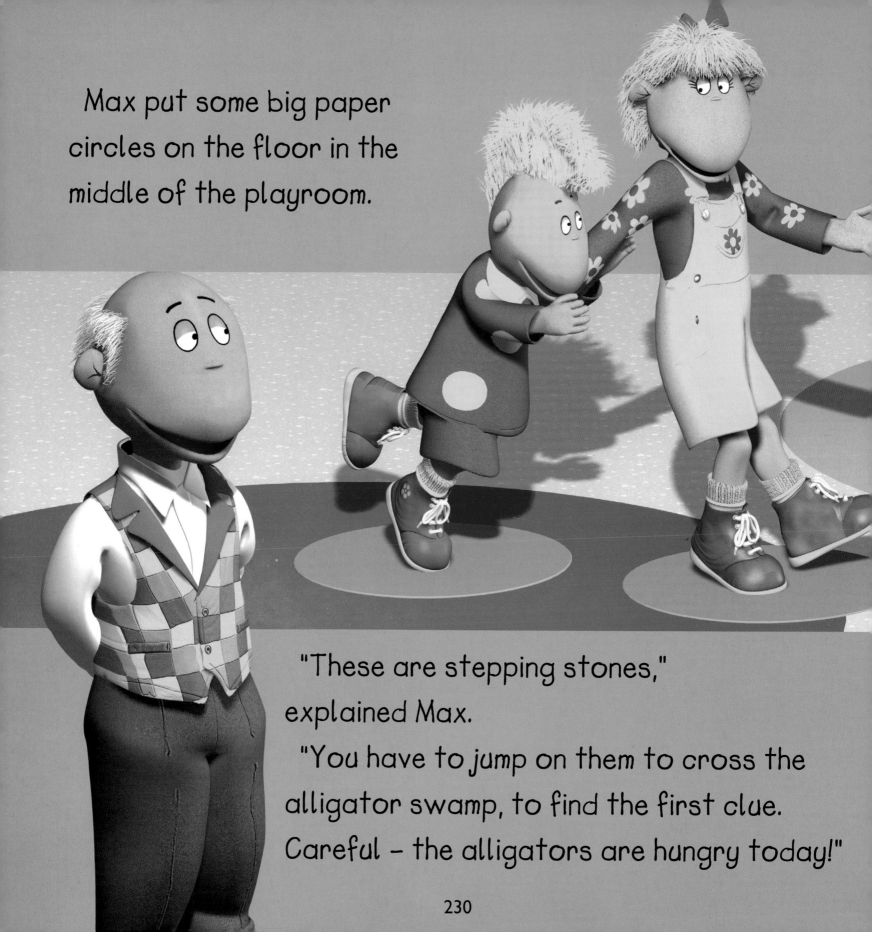

Max put some big paper circles on the floor in the middle of the playroom.

"These are stepping stones," explained Max.

"You have to jump on them to cross the alligator swamp, to find the first clue. Careful – the alligators are hungry today!"

Fizz squealed as she jumped onto the first stepping stone. Milo, Bella and Jake followed.
"Ow – I think something bit me," shouted Jake.

"It's all right, Jake. There aren't any real alligators," whispered Bella. The stepping stones led into the garden.

Max told them the first clue.

"I'm very colourful and you can climb up my steps to the top. The fun bit is when you whizz down again to the bottom. What am I?"

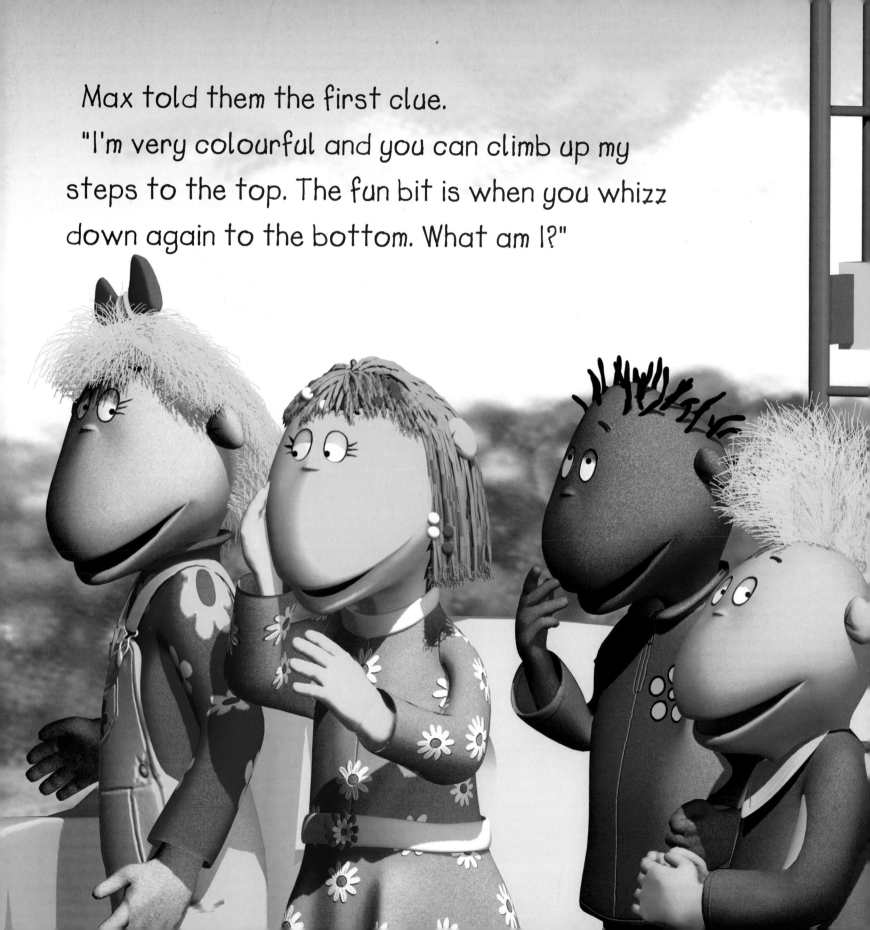

The Tweenies thought carefully.

"Something colourful," said Milo.

"With steps to climb up," added Bella.

"Oh, it's a hard clue," sighed Jake.

"I know, I know. You can whizz down it to the bottom. It must be...

...the slide on the climbing frame!" cried Fizz.

One by one, the Tweenies climbed up the steps of the climbing frame and whizzed down the slide, landing in a big heap at the bottom.

"What's the next clue, Max?" asked Milo, impatiently.

"Well," Max began. "The pink princess has been locked away at the top of the Green Tower. You have to rescue her and take her to the furry king and queen," he said, mysteriously.

"I know who the furry king and queen are," said Jake at once, spying Doodles and Izzles in a corner of the garden.

"But where's the Green Tower?" asked Fizz.

"It must be somewhere high up," decided Milo.

"Maybe the Green Tower is a...

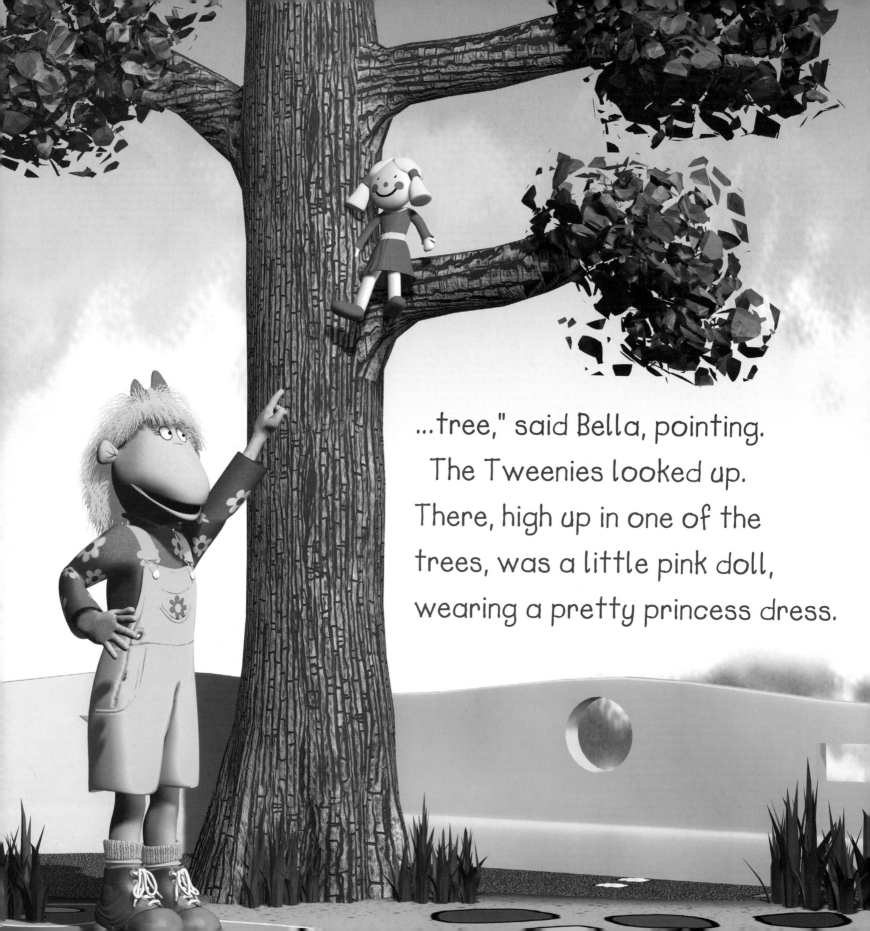

...tree," said Bella, pointing.
The Tweenies looked up.
There, high up in one of the
trees, was a little pink doll,
wearing a pretty princess dress.

"That must be the pink princess," said Bella.
"But how are we going to rescue her? It's so high up," wailed Jake.
"Why not try working together?" suggested Max.

"I've got an idea," said Fizz. "Jake's not very heavy. Milo can give him a piggy back and then he can reach up and grab the dolly, I mean the pink princess."

So Milo crouched down and Jake jumped up on his back.

"Hold on tight," said Milo.

"Ooooh, I feel a bit wobbly," said Jake.

Jake reached up as high as he could. At first he couldn't quite reach the doll, but with one last big stretch, he grabbed her and then handed her to Doodles and Izzles.

"Well done," said Max. "Are you ready for your next clue, now?"

"Oh, yes," said the Tweenies, all at once.

"Well, the next one's indoors. A very important picture was broken up into little pieces by a nasty goblin. You have to put it together again."

"Lots of little pieces?" wondered Bella.

"That make a picture?" thought Milo.

"I know," said Jake, spying a box on the floor. "It's this jigsaw puzzle."

"Hey, well done, Jakey," laughed Fizz.

They set to work and soon they had put all the pieces together. It was a picture of a house.

"Where's Max?" said Bella. "We need the next clue now."

"Maybe the house is a clue," said Milo, slowly.

The Tweenies looked up and there in the window of the playhouse were Doodles and Izzles, barking excitedly.

The Tweenies ran into the playhouse and...

...there was Max with the jellies.

"You've found your treasure," Max said.

"The fruit jellies are ready now," said Jake.

"Look, they're all wobbly!" laughed Milo.

"That was quick," said Fizz.

"Time passed quickly because we were enjoying ourselves," said Bella.

"Mmmm, I like treasure hunts," said Jake.

"Woof! So do we," said Doodles and Izzles.

THE END

Potato Prints

One sunny morning, Missy Hissy went for a walk all around the garden.

She told Orbie
how bright his
yellow and blue
house looked.

Orbie was
very pleased!

Bilbo was polishing his blue and white boat.

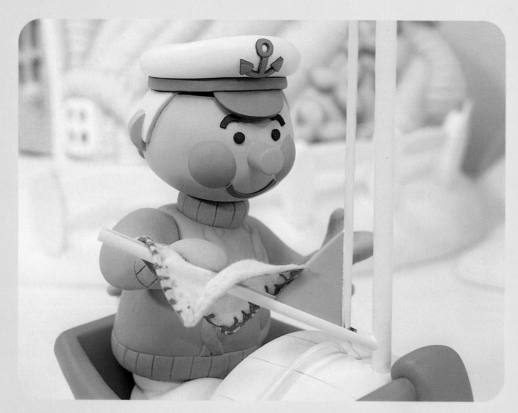

He was delighted when Missy Hissy said how smart it looked.

Then Missy Hissy told Tiffo she liked his
purple house. Tiffo wondered why Missy Hissy
looked so sad.

Missy Hissy looked at her drainpipes. They
weren't bright and colourful like her friends' houses.
Missy Hissy thought everyone had a nicer house
than she did.

Tiffo told Looby Loo that Missy Hissy was upset about something.

Looby Loo went to Missy Hissy's house to find out what was the matter.

Missy Hissy told Looby Loo that she was upset because all the houses in the garden were bright and colourful, except for her drainpipes.

Looby Loo went to ask Andy Pandy what they could do to help.

Andy Pandy said he had an idea. He'd help Missy Hissy with...
a potato!
Looby Loo was very puzzled.

Andy Pandy went to his special cupboard and got a knife, an old plate and some paints.

Then Andy Pandy asked Teddy if he wanted to come and help make Missy Hissy's house more colourful, using a potato.

Teddy was very puzzled.

Missy Hissy was pleased to see her friends. But
she was puzzled, too. How was a potato going to
make her house more colourful?

Andy Pandy said that was a secret.

Andy Pandy very carefully sliced the potato
in half.

Then, he asked Teddy to put some red paint on
the plate.

Andy Pandy told Teddy to dip the potato in the paint...and put it on Missy Hissy's drainpipes.

Teddy was amazed. The potato had made a
beautiful bright red print! Teddy started making
lots of potato prints on Missy Hissy's house.

Now it was Andy Pandy's turn. He put some blue paint on the plate, and dipped the other half of the potato in it.

Soon, Andy Pandy and Teddy had covered
Missy Hissy's drainpipes with red and blue
potato prints.

Missy Hissy thought her house looked
wonderful. She said thank you to Andy Pandy.
Then she said thank you to Teddy. Then she said
thank you to them both together!

Andy Pandy tidied away his things, and invited everyone to his house for tea.

"No, thank you!" said Missy Hissy. She wanted to stay in her bright and colourful house.

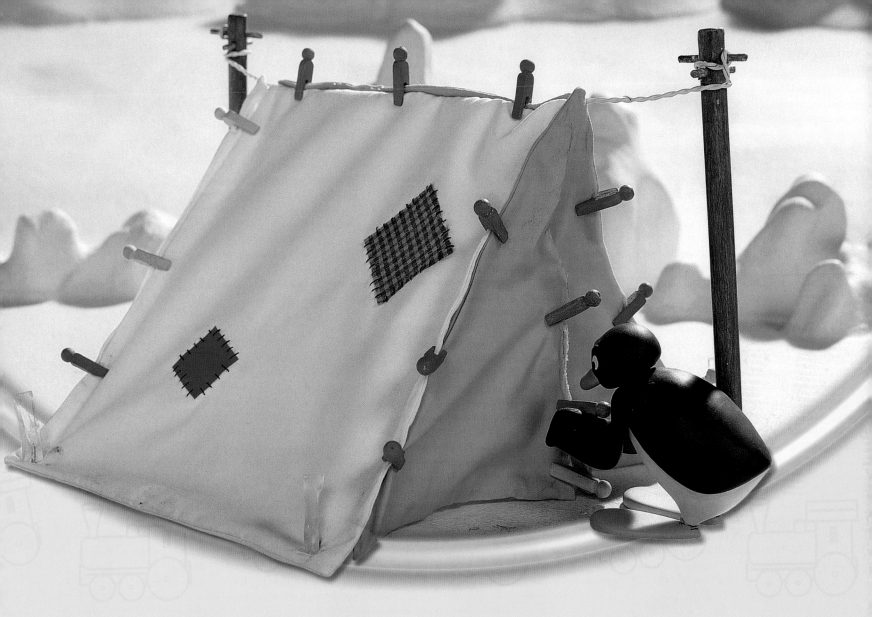

Pingu Goes Camping

Pingu and Pinga were trying to make a tent.

Father helped them to put it up, and brought some pillows to make the tent comfy.

Pingu said that he and Pinga were brave explorers and were going to camp out all night in the tent.

Pinga wanted her rabbit to camp out too, but Pingu didn't think that toy rabbits could be explorers.

But when Mother brought the brave explorers a basket of food, she brought Pinga's rabbit, too.

When it was time to get into bed, Pingu made scary faces at Pinga.

Then he
snatched
Pinga's rabbit
away from her, and pretended
it was a scary monster.

Pinga said that she didn't like her rabbit any more, and threw it out of the tent.

Now that Pinga had got rid of the rabbit, Pingu said that the explorers could go to sleep.

Suddenly,
there was a
strange crunch-
ing noise
from outside...

Then a big, scary shadow appeared on the side of the tent.

Pinga thought that her rabbit had come
to get them!
 Pingu told her not to be so silly and
that he wasn't scared at all.

Pinga said that if Pingu wasn't scared, he should go outside and find out what was making the noise and the shadow.

It wasn't Pinga's rabbit.

But Pingu could hear something eating their basket of food.

Pingu shone his torch in the direction of
the noise and revealed the monster…

It was Robby! He wanted
to camp out too.

Of course, Pingu had known all along that monsters didn't really exist!

Dizzy's Talkie Talkie

"Today," said Bob to Dizzy, "we need to collect rocks to make a platform for the new water tank, and build a water pump."

Just then, Wendy arrived on Scrambler.

"Welcome to our new home," said Bob.

"Wicked!" cried Scrambler. "Sunflower Valley rocks!"

"Here are the Talkie Talkies," said Wendy. "Now we can talk to each other in Sunflower Valley."

"Scrambler to Dizzy,
let's scram!" said Scrambler,
on his Talkie Talkie.

"Rock collecting, here
we come!" said Dizzy.

As Dizzy and Scrambler turned a corner, they saw a huge pile of rocks.

"Just what we need!" said Dizzy.

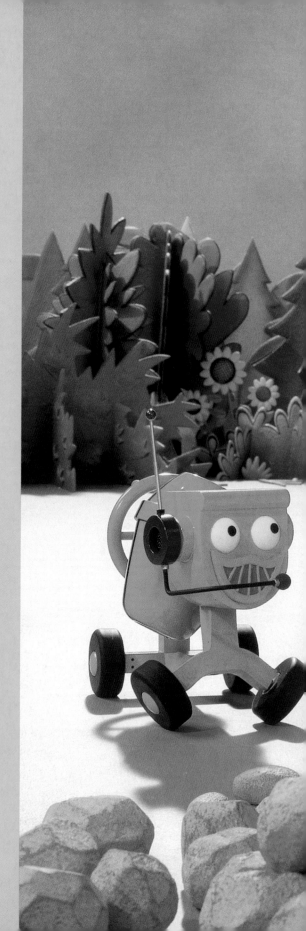

"Dizzy to Muck," said Dizzy through her Talkie Talkie. "We've found a huge pile of rocks!"

"Muck to Dizzy. On my way," replied Muck.

Back at the base,
Lofty was drilling a hole
for the pump for the
new water tank.

"That's it, Lofty," said
Bob. "The hole is nearly
deep enough."

Meanwhile, Dizzy and
Scrambler used the
Talkie Talkie system to
give Muck directions
to find them.

Muck and Scrambler picked up the rocks and transported them back to the base.

"Just what we need!" said Bob.

And they started to build the platform for the tank.

"A good job well done," said Bob when they had finished.

"Let's try out the pump," said Wendy.

The water flowed smoothly from the pump... and soaked poor Bob standing just below the tank!

"Whoaaaaa!" he shouted.

"Er, Dizzy to Bob!" giggled Dizzy through her Talkie Talkie, "You forgot to turn off the tap!"

BBC CHILDREN'S BOOKS
Published by the Penguin Group
Penguin Books Ltd, 80 Strand, London WC2R 0RL, England
Penguin Group (Australia), 250 Camberwell Road, Camberwell,
Victoria 3124, Australia (a division of Pearson Australia Group Pty Ltd)
Published by BBC Children's Books, 2006
Text and design © Children's Character Books, 2006
10 9 8 7 6 5 4 3 2 1
BBC & logo © and ™ BBC 1996
CBeebies & logo ™ BBC. © BBC 2002
All rights reserved.
ISBN 1 405 90315 5
ISBN 13: 9 78 1405 903158
Printed in China